The ABC's of
Planning Your Life

Dear Stefanie,

Thank you for all of
the love you share and
the passion you have for
the elderly and the young.
You are a teacher of so
much more than appears,
and you are such a gift!

Many blessings
to you.

Susan McLaughlin

The ABC's of
Planning Your Life

WHEN LIFE DOESN'T GO ACCORDING TO THE PLAN

LYNN MCLAUGHLIN

TATE PUBLISHING
AND ENTERPRISES, LLC

Published by Tate Publishing & Enterprises, LLC
127 E. Trade Center Terrace | Mustang, Oklahoma 73064 USA
1.888.361.9473 | www.tatepublishing.com

Tate Publishing is committed to excellence in the publishing industry. The company reflects the philosophy established by the founders, based on Psalm 68:11,
"The Lord gave the word and great was the company of those who published it."

Book design copyright © 2014 by Tate Publishing, LLC. All rights reserved.
Cover design by Nikolai Purpura
Cover artist Dani McGrath
Interior design by Joana Quilantang

Published in the United States of America

ISBN: 978-1-63367-374-8
Poetry / Subjects & Themes / Inspirational & Religious
14.09.30

So what is it about the plan? I was not aware that I actually had a plan, until things began to happen that were not a part of the plan!

What I have come to realize is that there is a master plan. I am not the planner, nor am I the master of the plan. Yet, it is the plan that is mine. It is called "life".

I have been given a life to find joy and happiness that can only be chosen by me. It is in my joy, my love of my life, my love for and acceptance of the love of my creator, that I can be a light and inspiration to others to live their lives fully.

This book is written with love and dedication to my creator, whom I refer to as God, the Gift Of Divinity that lives within me.

Acknowledge God first, in All things.[1]

---

[1] In all your ways acknowledge Him first And He shall direct your paths.

Proverbs 3:6

B

Believe that you were made in his likeness and image.[2]

---

[2] Then God said, Let Us make man in Our image, according to Our likeness.

Genesis 1:26

Believe in the Lord your God, and you shall be established.

2 Ch 20:20

C

Choose you this day. Who will you serve?[3]

---

[3]   No one can serve two masters; for either he will hate the one and love the other, or else he will be loyal to the one and despise the other. You cannot serve God and mammon.

Matthew 6:24

D

Deliver God
By
Delivering yourself
From Doubt.[4]

---

[4] He trusted in the Lord, let Him rescue Him; Let Him deliver Him, since He delights in Him!

Psalm 22:8

Experience God in Everything you do and with Everyone you meet.[5]

---

[5]   Jesus said to them, "If God were your Father, you would love Me, for I proceeded forth and came from God; nor have I come of Myself, but he sent Me.

John 8:42

First acknowledge God within yourself Followed by acknowledging God in everyone you meet.[6]

---

[6]   I and My Father are one.

John 10:30

One God and Father of all, who is above all, and through all, and in you all.

Ephesians 4:6

G

Giving God Experiences by Giving the Gifts You were Given By God.[7]

---

[7]   As each one has received a gift, minister it to one another, as good stewards of the manifold grace of God.

1 Peter 4:10

Happiness is what Happens when you share who you really are.

Who am I?[8]

---

[8] Delight yourself also in the Lord, and He shall give you the desires of your heart.

Psalm 37:4

I

I am the
I am.
Inside of this
body is where
I live.
What **I** express to
the world is who
I believe **I** am.[9]

---

[9] I am the vine, you are the branches. He who abides in Me, and
I in him, bears much fruit; for without Me you can do nothing.

John 15:5

J

It's Just about me,
it's Just about you.
Jesus was Just a man,
Just like me and you.
What did Jesus know
that we don't?[10]

---

[10] All things were made through Him, and without Him nothing was made that was made.

John 1:3

K

Know?
Jesus **K**new that it was not him who doeth the work. It was his Father working through him. All those years ago Jesus **K**new the answer.[11]

---

[11] Do you not believe that I am in the Father, and the Father in Me? The words that I speak to you I do not speak on my own authority; but the Father who dwells in me does the works.

John 14:10

L

Love
Live to Love your
Life with no
Limits to your
Love.
Learn about who
you really are,
Letting everyone be per-
suaded by their own mind.[12]

---

[12] One person esteems one day above another; another esteems every day alike. Let each be fully convinced in his own mind.

Romans 14:5

Man was
Made in the
likeness and image
of our creator.
My Mind Makes
Me the Master of
My life when the
Memory of My Maker
is what Moves Me.[13]

---

[13] Trust in the Lord with all your heart, And lean not on your own understanding; In all your ways acknowledge Him, And He shall direct your paths.

Proverbs 3:5-6

N

No matter how it
appears there is
No thing,
No person,
No situation
that God hasn't got.[14]

---

[14] And we know that all things work together for good to those
who love God, to those who are called according to His purpose.

Romans 8:28

Overcoming every thing, every person, every situation, and every **O**bstacle is what happens when I give all of my concerns **O**ver to my creator.[15]

---

[15] What then shall we say to these things? If God is for us, who can be against us?

Romans 8:31

P

Present the **P**erson
who was created
to be the **P**resent
to this world.[16]

---

[16]   For we are His workmanship, created in Christ Jesus for good
       works, which God prepared beforehand that we should walk
       in them.

Ephesians 2:10

Q

Questions can only exist because the answer lies within. If this were not the case, how would you know to ask the **Q**uestion? Where does God Live?[17]

---

[17]   Or do you not know that your body is the temple of the Holy Spirit who is in you, whom you have from God, and you are not your own?

1 Corinthians 6:19

R

Remember where
you came from.
Remember
who you are.
Remember who
doeth the work.[18]

---

[18] Every good gift and every perfect gift is from above, and comes down from the Father of lights, with whom there is no variation or shadow of turning.

James 1:17

S

Show the world
Someone **S**pecial.
Share **S**omething
with **S**omeone.
Simply **S**mile![19]

---

[19] Happy are the people who are in such a state; Happy are the
people whose God is the Lord!

Psalm 144:15

T

Tell the **T**ruth
Take the **T**ime
Trust that **T**ruth
is who you are.
It will make
you free.[20]

---

[20] And you shall know the truth, and the truth shall make you free.

John 8:32

U

Understand that
when you
Underestimate who
you are, you are being
Ungrateful to
the One who created
you as **U**s.[21]

---

[21] For I rejoiced greatly when brethren came and testified of the truth that is in you, just as you walk in the truth. I have no greater joy than to hear that my children walk in truth.

John 3:3–4

Visit the place within, being Very quiet and Very still.[22]

---

[22]   But the Lord is in His holy temple. Let all the earth keep silence before Him.

Habakkuk 2:20

Or do you not know that your body is the temple of the Holy Spirit who is in you, whom you have from God, and you are not your own?

1 Corinthians 6:19

"Be still, and know that I am God;"

Psalm 46:10

With all your heart,
With all your soul,
know that you can
Withstand anything
because of
What lies Within.[23]

---

[23] I will say of the Lord, "He is my refuge and my fortress; My God, in Him I will trust."

Psalm 91:2

It's
All
Good![24]

You
are
Good!²⁵

---

²⁵ *Take your pen and make an X through one of the "O's" in the word "good".

Z

Zest for Life!
Zest for Love!²⁶

---

26   Delight yourself also in the Lord, And He shall give you the desires of your heart.

Psalm 37:4

This is the day the Lord has made; We will rejoice and be glad in it.

Psalm 118:24